Eastern White Pine
Birch
Beech
Tulip Poplar
Black Walnut
Douglas Fir
White Oak
Red Maple
Sassafras
Ginkgo

For my sister Janet

 Printed in the United States of America. For information address HarperCollins Children's Books, a division of HarperCollins Publishers, 195 Broadway, New York, NY 10007. www.harpercollinschildrens.com. Watercolors, acrylic paint, gouache, and digital collage were used to create the illustrations. The text type is Belizio.

Library of Congress Cataloging-in-Publication Data
Names: Hesselberth, Joyce, author. Title: Beatrice was a tree / Joyce Hesselberth.
Description: First edition. | New York, NY : Greenwillow Books, an imprint of HarperCollins Publishers, [2021] | Audience: Ages 4-8. | Audience: Grades K-1. | Summary: A young girl named Beatrice imagines herself as a tree and envisions how she would interact with her natural surroundings and change throughout the seasons. Includes factual information on trees and photosynthesis.
Identifiers: LCCN 2020047367 | ISBN 9780062741264 (hardback)
Subjects: CYAC: Trees—Fiction. | Imagination—Fiction.
Classification: LCC PZ7.1.H53 Be 2021 | DDC [E]—dc23
LC record available at https://lccn.loc.gov/2020047367
21 22 23 24 25 PC 10 9 8 7 6 5 4 3 2 1 First Edition   Greenwillow Books

Greenwillow Books
An Imprint of HarperCollins*Publishers*

BEATRICE,
TIME FOR BED!

"If I were a tree,"
said Beatrice, "I could
stay outside all night long."

"If I were a tree," Beatrice whispered,

“I would have a trunk, and bark, and branches and leaves. Lots of leaves.”

Darkness fell. Stars sparkled. Beatrice swayed in the breeze.

All night long, until . . .

Tweet! Chirp! Caw-caw! Tsk, tsk!
The dawn chorus began.

Beatrice stretched her limbs
to catch the morning sun.

Birds made their homes in her branches.
She cradled a tiny, perfect nest full of tiny,
perfect eggs.

Squirrels climbed up, up, up her trunk.
They chattered and scolded, jumping
from branch to branch.
Beatrice bounced and shook her leaves.

Caterpillars gnawed.
Deer nibbled.
Spiders spun.
Owl slept.

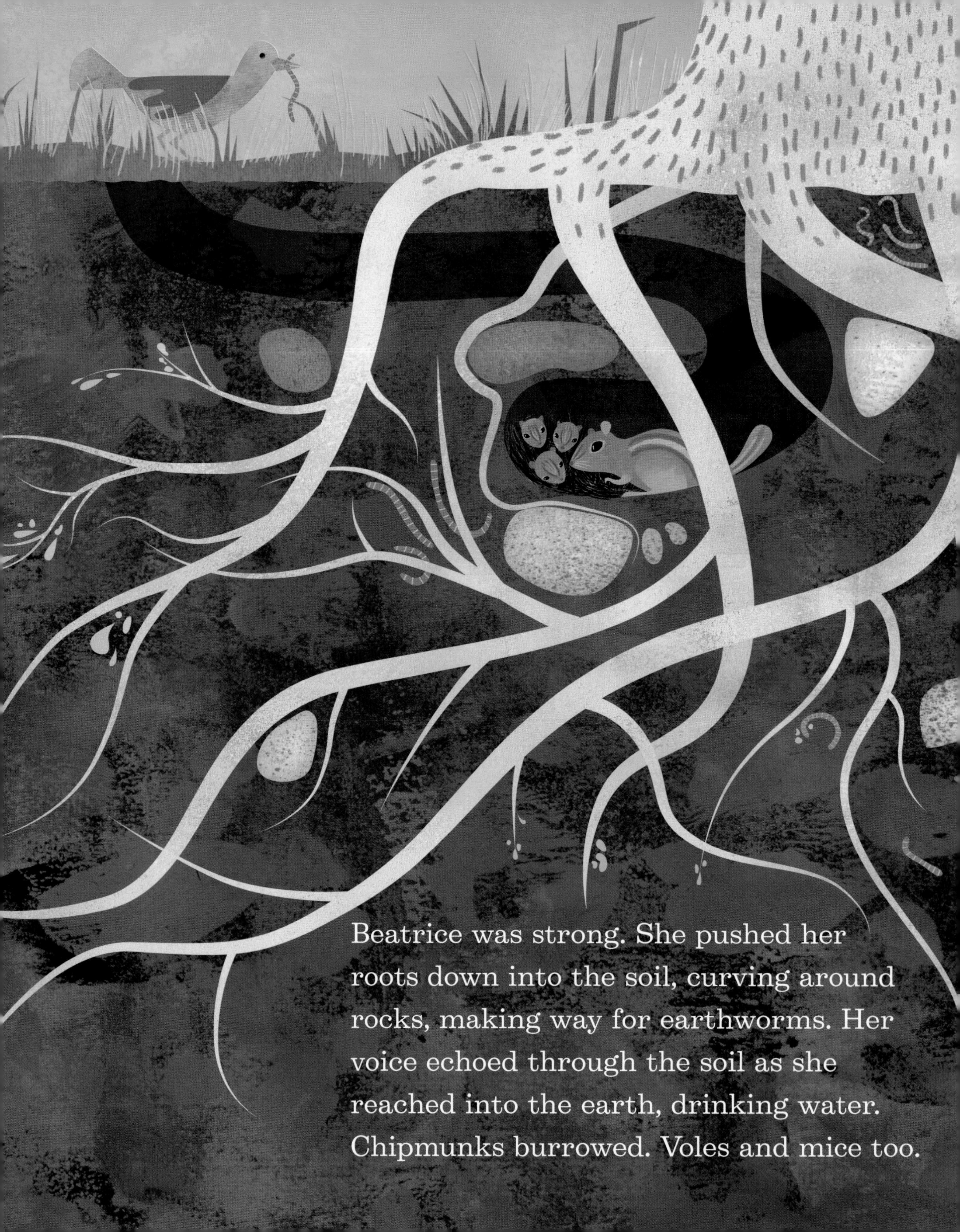

Beatrice was strong. She pushed her roots down into the soil, curving around rocks, making way for earthworms. Her voice echoed through the soil as she reached into the earth, drinking water. Chipmunks burrowed. Voles and mice too.

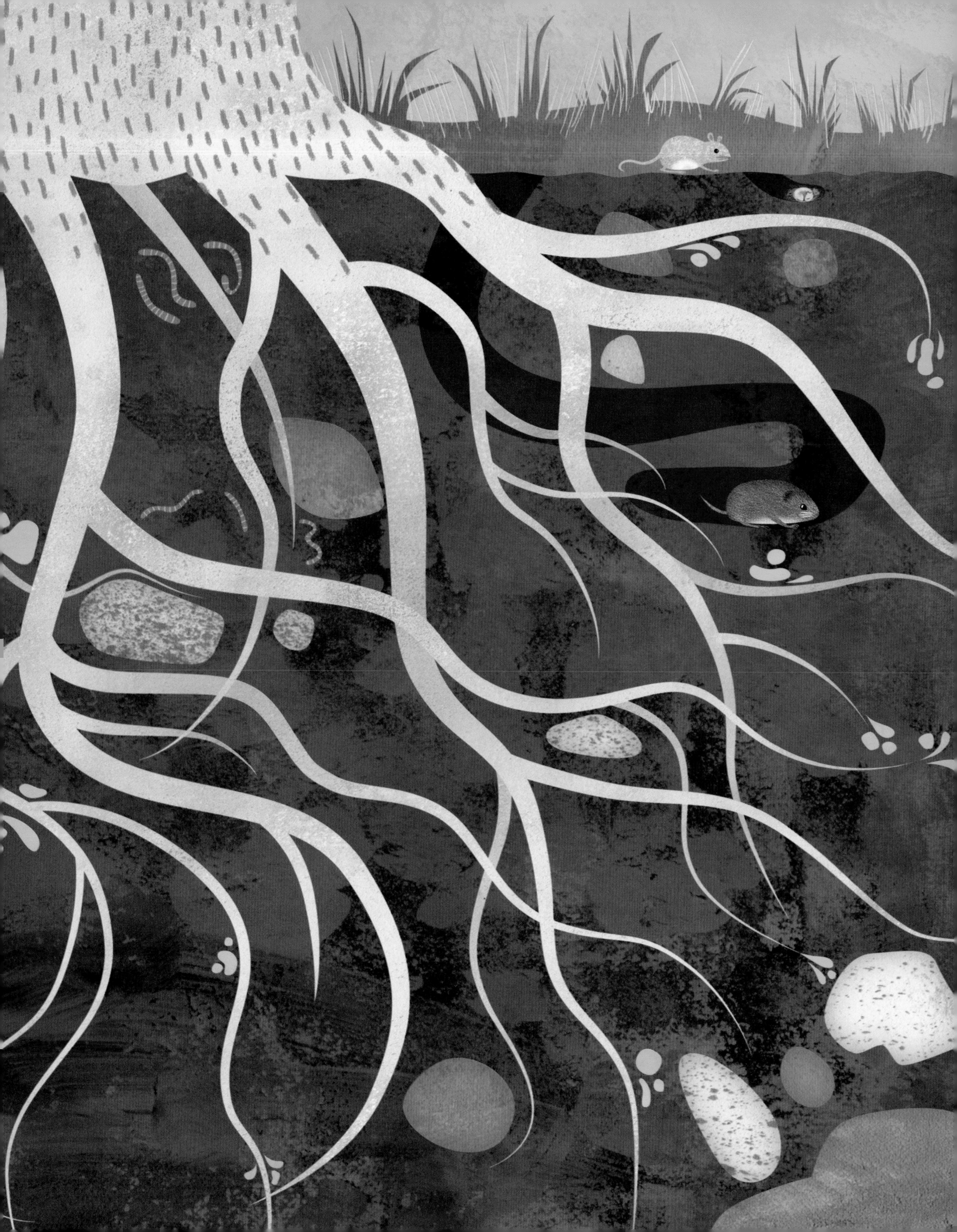

The air turned sweet and crisp. Beatrice's leaves put on a magic show as summer turned to fall.

"Goodbye, goodbye, goodbye," whispered Beatrice, as her leaves twisted and twirled and sailed away.

Until they were gone.

Beatrice waited.
Snow fell.
Ice dripped.
Rabbit nibbled.
Quiet.

And then, one day when she couldn't wait anymore, Beatrice bloomed.

It was spring.

BEATRICE,
BED! NOW!

What Makes a Tree?

How Do Animals Use Trees?

Many animals and insects make their homes in or near trees. Animals and insects also use trees for food. Did you spot any of these animals in the story? What other animals need trees?

- Birds
- Squirrels
- Deer
- Caterpillars
- Flies
- Voles
- Chipmunks
- Worms
- Bees
- Butterflies
- Spiders
- Mice

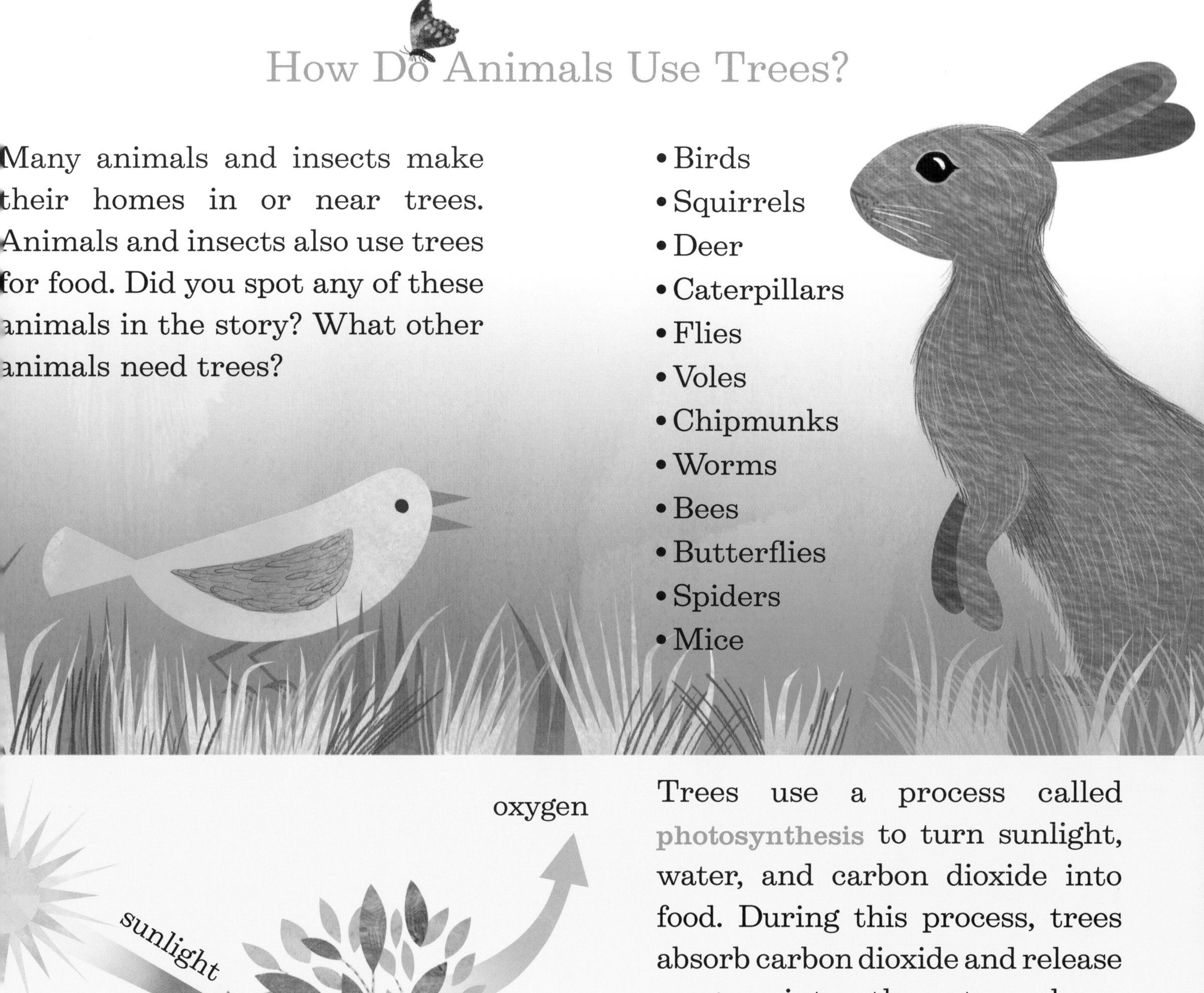

Trees use a process called **photosynthesis** to turn sunlight, water, and carbon dioxide into food. During this process, trees absorb carbon dioxide and release oxygen into the atmosphere. Trees add more oxygen to the air, for animals and humans to breathe. So . . . PLANT A TREE! You'll be making the world a better place to live.

Eastern White Pine
Sassafras
Beech
Birch
Tulip Poplar
White Oak
Black Walnut
Douglas Fir
Red Maple
Ginkgo